Edward's Portrait

STORY AND PICTURES BY

BARBARA MORROW

Macmillan Publishing Company   New York
Collier Macmillan Canada   Toronto
Maxwell Macmillan International Publishing Group
New York   Oxford   Singapore   Sydney

Macmillan Publishing Company, 866 Third Avenue, New York, NY 10022. Collier Macmillan Canada, Inc., 1200 Eglinton Avenue East, Suite 200, Don Mills, Ontario M3C 3N1. First edition. Printed in Singapore.

10 9 8 7 6 5 4 3 2 1

The text of this book is set in 16 point Fournier. The illustrations are rendered in watercolor and pencil.

Library of Congress Cataloging-in-Publication Data. Morrow, Barbara. Edward's portrait : story and pictures / by Barbara Morrow. — 1st ed.   p.   cm. Summary: A family has individual daguerreotype portraits taken in the earliest days of photography. ISBN 0-02-767591-2 [1. Photography—Fiction.] I. title. PZ7.M84535Ed 1991 [E]—dc20 90-45008

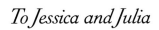

To Jessica and Julia

"Here comes Pa," Edward said from his place by the window. "He's running."

Ma looked up from her biscuit making. "My!" she said. "He looks excited."

Pa burst in, waving the *Weekly Clarion*. "Listen to this," he shouted.

"It says here: 'On or about June the twelfth, Mr. J. Fitzpatrick, daguerreotypist, will set up his traveling gallery in the lot behind the hotel. Daguerreotype portraits will be taken. Priced one dollar and upward. Children welcome.' And he's here right on schedule!" said Pa.

Ma and Edward looked at the notice in the newspaper.

"What is a duh-gehr-uh-type?" Edward asked.

"It's a perfect little picture of a person or a place," said Ma. "No one painted it with a brush. No one drew it with a pen or pencil. It's like magic!"

"Yes, like magic," Pa agreed. "The picture appears when light is focused upon a plate of silver-coated copper inside a box called a camera. The tube at the front of the camera is aimed at the person or scene for one or two minutes, sometimes longer. Then the box is taken into a dark place, where the copper plate is removed and treated with certain chemicals. And, presto! The picture is there for all to see."

"Oh," said Edward.

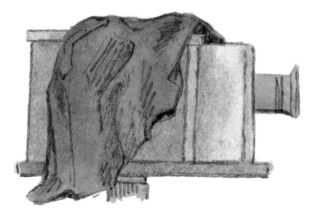

"The picture is framed in a beautiful little case you can hold in your hand or display on the parlor table. And you can keep it forever," Ma said dreamily.

"By Jove!" Pa said. "We ought to have our pictures taken."

Ma agreed, but Edward wasn't so sure. How could he possibly stand still for a whole minute or two? And he couldn't imagine baby Lucy sitting quietly unless she was asleep.

Edward squirmed while Ma brushed his hair, and fidgeted while she tied the bow of his best shirt.

"Now, Edward," Ma said, "you want to look nice to have your picture taken, don't you?"

"No," Edward whispered.

But Ma gave a last tug to the bow, and straightening her bonnet, she took Edward's hand to join Pa and Lucy for the trip to Mr. Fitzpatrick's traveling gallery.

"My, isn't it grand!" Ma said when they came in sight of the wagon, brightly painted with signs and pictures, and with a large window on one side.

Mr. Fitzpatrick opened the door. "Shall we do this young man first?" he said, patting Edward on the head.

Edward moved closer to Ma. "I don't want to," he said.

So Pa said he would be first. He sat in the chair offered to him, and Mr. Fitzpatrick pushed a queer iron thing behind the chair.

To Edward's horror, he placed Pa's head in it and turned a screw.

"This headrest is just to help you hold your head still, sir. It will take a while to make the picture," said Mr. Fitzpatrick. With that he ducked under a black cloth draped over the camera, explaining, "I can see better what the picture will be like if I am in the dark. It's almost as if I were inside the camera."

Pa sat and stared straight ahead. Edward held his breath. But nothing seemed to be happening.

At last Mr. Fitzpatrick came out of hiding. "That's all, sir," he said, loosening the headrest. "Now let's do the lady."

Ma handed Lucy to Pa and took her turn in the chair.

After Ma, Lucy had her picture taken—tied in a chair with a pillow behind her.

Then it was Edward's turn. "I don't want to," he yelled. "I don't want to be tied in a chair. I don't want to have my head in that thing."

"Now, Edward," Ma said.

"*Edward!*" Pa said.

"I'll tell you what, young feller," said Mr. Fitzpatrick. "If you will stand there quietly and let me put your head in this rest, I'll tell you about my travels to the lands of the Indian nation to take pictures of the warriors there."

So Edward let Mr. Fitzpatrick pose him in front of the camera, and Mr. Fitzpatrick began: "I traveled on the rivers and on the rails—*hold still, now!*" he warned.

Edward held still, and tried to imagine boats and trains.

"I bumped across the flowery prairie in my wagon—*steady, now!*" said Mr. Fitzpatrick.

Edward stared at the camera without blinking, and thought of Mr. Fitzpatrick bouncing in his beautiful wagon.

"I came at last to an Indian camp. The Indians crowded around my wagon, pointing and exclaiming. I showed them some of my pictures and my camera. But when I asked them to pose for me, they would not. They were afraid of the iron head-rest and of the camera pointing at them—*don't move!*" cried Mr. Fitzpatrick.

Edward held his breath, and sympathized with the Indians.

Mr. Fitzpatrick returned to his story. "At last the chief said he would have his picture made. He held his bow and his arrows and his spear. He looked very brave and fierce, and I made a fine picture of him—*ho-o-ld it, young feller!*"

Edward wished he had a bow and some arrows. And a spear.

Just when Edward thought he might burst, Mr. Fitzpatrick cried, "Finished!" and unscrewed the headrest.

As he disappeared behind a curtain, Mr. Fitzpatrick said, "Make yourselves comfortable, folks. In a few minutes you will have your pictures."

When he returned, he handed Pa and Ma what looked like four little black books, each fastened shut with a clasp.

They opened them one by one. As if by magic, in the first one was Pa. In the second was Ma. In the third was Lucy.

And there, in the last one, was Edward, looking as brave and fierce as an Indian chief.